Gallery Books
Editor: Peter Fallon

THE GHOST TRAIN

Frank Ormsby

THE GHOST TRAIN

Gallery Books

The Ghost Train
is first published
simultaneously in paperback
and in a clothbound edition
on 31 October 1995.

The Gallery Press
Loughcrew
Oldcastle
County Meath
Ireland

ISBN 1 85235 172 1 (*paperback*)
     1 85235 173 X (*clothbound*)

The Gallery Press receives financial assistance from An Chomhairle
Ealaíon / The Arts Council, Ireland, and acknowledges also the assistance of The Arts Council of Northern Ireland in the publication of
this book.

Contents

for Karen and Helen

Helen Keller

Brighter than gold trumpets, swords of light,
tougher than mailed fist or splendid spur
and softer than pelts in young fur-traders' hands.

White as the white wings lifting from the ark,
those fingers moving in a soundless dark.

The Ghost Train

The dawn train passes under King William Park,
shuddering the clay platforms of the dead.
Down with the cholera victims, rushing through
a mass grave from another century,
we cannot tell which ghosts are obsolete
or which may yet come sighing from the walls
with a glimmer of recognition
to take their place by more immediate shades:
parents and wives and children and the selves
we think of as dead.

An arch of day. We rattle into the sun
a birth-cry from the maternity clinic's door.
It may be that by accidents of birth
we haunt those children's futures,
that they are aboard,
or, weightless still, stationed in waiting rooms
at unknown junctions.
By mid-day they may have huddled about the knees
in the first carriage,
hostile or friendly as the way decrees
or latent with the forever
it may take them to come to us, for us
to lurk or nestle in their invisible baggage.

Dusk, and we queue again to take our places.
Burdened, neutral, or still travelling light,
past clinic windows, under King William Park,
we bring to platforms only partly home
more than our substance, more than our visible selves.

Geography

for Neil Johnston

1

Ireland, the World, the Universe
orbiting the walls of Whitehill Primary.
Counties and countries. Cosmic marbles hung
between sky-grey windows.
The Lower Infants' pre-Copernican doze
under bangled Saturn.

Signals drift to you from another world
beyond the big curtain where letters join
and the language is different. Multiply. Divide.
Sent on an errand there, you might return
startled to new perspectives: a football Moon,
the shared red of Mars and Africa.

Or wake in the North Atlantic, bumping ashore
on a shape in named fragments that magnifies
the World's tints and shadings.
A wild surmise.
Strike inland till you find it, your home place,
brown as the Matto Grosso, its two loughs slung
between Baltic Cavan, steppe-green Donegal.

2

Cavehill to Cassiopeia, the tireless eyes
of the Black Mountain transmitter. Forty years on,
I'm peering north in the Belfast night sky
for Sergei Krikalyov's fretful Muscovite face
at his bedsit window, stuck between here and the stars.
Once there was Russia, once a reliable earth
as fixed as the Urals. Now, soviets groaning apart.
Weightless, half-homeless, past his splash-down date,
Sergei adjusts his dials, in range at last
of all he knows for now of the once-known world.
My ear cocked like a satellite dish, I hear
Hiberno-English cut from west of the Bann
across the crackle of the universe. Manus is on the air.
Manus McClafferty, somewhere in Donegal,
to Sergei Krikalyov: 'How's she cuttin', boy?'
(Or did I imagine that?) and Sergei replies:
'It's a hard oul' station, Manus, but what can you do?'
Whatever they say, it warms the infinite sky
for the space of three minutes. He basks again
in the temperature of greetings, world restored
by the weight of a local accent. When his own voice
re-enters the atmosphere at Doochary or Loughanure,
it's as good as a night out, a dander in space.
He overtakes a tractor on main street Gweedore
and hurtles through Glenties. Already he has become
(Crockallyove, Kirklove, Crackallyev) a shifting shape
in border folklore, the stranger and guest star
in yarns of the Blue Stack Mountains, extravagant tales
from the Atlantic seaboard. And Georgia is Donegal
and Donegal the coast of Estonia, where he too re-shapes
his place on the planet, the geography of home.

Roslea Hero

*Winner of the All-Ireland
Donkey Derby at Clabby,
County Fermanagh, 1957, 1958, 1960*

They should name a shrub after him, where he lies
under the Murrays' garden in Derryard,
some hardy annual with a local strain
that roots among mountains, skirts the Border roads
where he slogged into Monaghan under a sack of flour
and home in the evening between two crates of eggs.
Its blossom should flare punctually on August days
with a scent of victory, a Clabby asphodel
sprung from whatever underground he shares
with Swift Swallow, Flying Saucer, Paddy the Egg —
unlikely hero who scampered into myth
on somebody's hayfield, leased for an afternoon,
head winged, heels flying, drawing us all behind,
the pride of the Border counties, crossing the line.

The All-Ireland Campaign

The day the Loughsiders played the Oak Leaf Boys
in the Ulster Championship
the forwards left their shooting boots at home.
Ball after ball flew wide at the Bridge Street end
or bounced on the pavilion roof into the backyards
of watching families.

Under the tricolour, where reporters groaned
and stabbed their notebooks, I dreamed of cavalcades:
a resurrection pageant streaming south
one autumn Sunday till not a soul was left
from Brookeborough to the Border,
and afterwards a rapturous progress north,
horns blaring, lights blazing the length of Ireland.

The Loughsiders went under. A thousand times
I dived into the bottom of the deep
to pluck up drowned honour. Or, point by point,
rehearsed the next All-Ireland campaign.
Fear in the Orchard County, sleepless nights
from Breffni to the homes of Donegal.
My cultured left foot and my cultured right
guiding the Loughsiders into the second round.

One Saturday

1

Nose close to the handlebars, bum in the air
like Scobie Breasley,
I'm home from McBride's betting-shop in time
for starter's orders.

Sweet Little Volga Boatman is the one
my father's modest hopes are riding on,
a shilling each way.
                        Speechless since his stroke,
suddenly he trails a rein of saliva.
If his legs would take the strain
he'd be skelping his buttocks the length of the home straight.

2

And a beast, some humped blackness, heaves its head,
the ox in Uttoxeter finding form at last
in troubled light on a Saturday afternoon.

3

Before the commentator's *How they finished*, before he can
    slow
to word-pictures of an enclosure,
I'm in the saddle again, away at full stretch
to collect our winnings.

But carrying now the weight, the dead weight
of that baffled mobility.

The Gatecrasher

On the lookout for my father in his prime,
I catch him, head down, affecting a bowler,
in John Lavery's *The Weighing Room, Hurst Park*.

He can hardly believe his luck. An hour ago
he dropped his scythe discreetly in the long grass
of a Fermanagh farm, now he is half a length

from that frail figure, poised, posed in the scales.
In a minute he will step forward, paunch drawn in,
to shake the hand of the boul' Steve Donoghue.

More likely, he'll lose his nerve. More likely still,
those two stewards who have begun to enquire
will show him — there's no justice — the weighing room door.

Before he is turfed out, I hope he takes time
to commend the artist ('You're doing rightly, sur.')
or, as though it might tip the balance, touch him once,

speculatively, on the shoulder, as the jockeys do.

Reading to my Father

1

Mostly the random poetry of horses' names,
their odds, jockeys, trainers, how they fared
on the last outing. You listened with a blurred,
half-elsewhere look, unbroken and unlamed
briefly, something intact and surging clear
that had chafed under starters' orders.

2

Listen, I've found the pages. *The Irish News*,
June, 1960, the runners starting on time,
on those lost days between your heart's last flutter
and your box reined clumsily into the ground.

I stop when you touch my arm. Paddy's Chance
in the 2.30. Again at Western Sky
and Terra Nova. You raise the ghost of a smile
for Judgement, Poetic Licence, Lucky Guy.

3

Print darkens my fingers, weeks, then years.
Hundreds of winners, thousands of also-rans
at full tilt, outdistancing that June,
its hobblers and fallers. They carry me again
beyond the fact of your death. Outstrip once more
those weightless hours, paceless afternoons:
at 3.00, at 3.30 the wireless set
in its boxed, terrible silence.

Picking Winners

1

Their names on strips of paper, flung to the wind.
Which was the winner? Was the first to ground
valued for speed, or due an early fall?
Last down the one for distances, or doomed
to a riderless meander?

Whatever the rules, all morning we pursued
the afternoon's impending secrets. Sunk in an easy chair
my father weighed the outcome gravely,
the breeze his oracle, chance a veiled pattern
as close as the sky.

2

All this a dim mosaic come to light
on the floors of memory,
its blank squares and random spaces filled
with favourites, dark horses on trial runs.
Like scraps of an old myth that might cohere,
they have slipped the dull harness of time and place:
names on strips of paper flung to the wind
are falling as ghostly snow in lost corners
of the next townland, or light years away —
Little Horse, Winged Horse — in sparkling form still

among the constellations.

Winter Sports

Crossing the line on the Enniskillen road
where Tyrone becomes Fermanagh,
the Oaks the St Leger,
the Cesarewitch the 2,000 Guineas,
we find we've exhausted the classics.

Time for our photo-finish: a framed glow
from the kitchen window,
us piddling white horses in a bank of snow.

Action Replays

for my brother Seamus

1

Tired of ice, the flawed mintage
chipped from our buckets,
drips spiking the eaves,

we take to the snowfields,
cantering on the trail
of a jockey named Winter.

Chepstow and Market Rasen
run in our heads,
the sound of Wincanton:

racecourse England,
its thunderous afternoons
of furlongs and fences.

We are the 3.30, a two-horse race
through Donnelly's Bottom.
When we lap

the 4 o'clock, already our sights are set
on the 4.40 before darkness falls,
the next stumbling freeze.

2

That day you stumbled off the scaffolding,
you fell with a jockey's instinct, rolling clear,
remounted. The dark stayer timing its run
that trailed our father thirty years before
took ten days to catch you.
                              Now you walk
the backroads, day in day out, as though to stop
might ground you forever:
                              I flog the tired horse
of old endeavours, dreaming it might yet clear
your memory's blurred fences or, bolting, alarm
the least twitch in the nerves of a dead arm.

The Gap on my Shelf

Smaller than life, episcopal in death,
he lies, brows frowning
the length of his body,
the *Poems* of Mrs Hemans under his chin.

The lips sink in his face, his paunch settles
as the hump of a grave levels at last with the earth.
Empty of self, he fills us with the tug
and ebb of his absence.

Where has he gone? When I try to imagine his soul
in flight before dawn or fluttering down at last
on the clouds of a catechism heaven,

what floods my head is dislocated light
and rain at the window,
some no-place, like the space where yesterdays go:

all I can see, the book-size gap on my shelf,
wordless with loss, where poems used to be.

The Sons

Carrying her to join him
they are borne
back to the start:
the dark corner
where they were conceived
under the Sacred Heart.

At Stoke Poges

To be stopped short by death here of all places.
Centuries of silence gather at the graves
of four schoolboys swept on a spring day
off the rocks at Land's End.
                                    And we who had come,
heads full of sad iambics, to the poet's tomb,
leave with their names by heart:
James Holloway, Robert Ankers, Ricci Lamden, Nicholas
    Hurst,
side by side on the brink of their lost teens
in the earth at Stoke Poges.

The Graveyard School

Life is no laughing matter. We entered crying
and Melancholy marked us for her own.
Our birth-day was the day we started dying.

Urn-shaped our souls, our fate to wander sighing
where names grow weathered, angels droop in stone.
Life is no laughing matter. We entered crying.

Sepulchral shades, the population lying
under our feet are kindred to the bone.
Our birth-day was the day we started dying.

What are our bodies? Houses putrefying,
clay tenements we moulder in alone.
Life is no laughing matter. We entered crying.

What is our song? A night-piece amplifying
owls in the yews, the universal groan.
Our birth-day was the day we started dying.

Your smile's a death-mask rictus. No denying
what we among the tombs have ever known:
Life is no laughing matter. We entered crying.
Our birth-day was the day we started dying.

from *The Memoirs*

after François Vidocq

Dunkirk, Calais, Ostend. Three times I tried
to embark for the New World. The fares were too high,
the captains unsympathetic. Instead I joined
the Paillasse of the famous Cotte-Comus,

where first I was master of lamps and chandeliers
and cleaned the cages (the tallow disgusted me,
the monkeys went for my eyes),
then failed trainee-tumbler. For three weeks

(the monkey's leap, the drunkard's leap, the coward's leap,
the chair-leap, the grand fling) I collected bruises,
aches, thrashings, a broken nose. Till Garnier said:
'I like you. You are dirty. Your flesh smells.

You are skeletal. Here is a tiger-skin and club.
From today you are a savage of the South Seas,
who eats raw flesh and cracks flints in his mouth
when he is thirsty. I want you to roll your eyes

and model your walk on the orang-utan
in cage number one.' A jar full of round stones
was set at my feet, also a live cock
with its legs tied. 'Gnaw this,' says Garnier.

'Like fuck I will.' I went for him with a stake
and the whole troupe fell on me with kicks and blows.
That night — homeless, broke — I headed for Arras
and my forgiving mother. I was now seventeen.

In Retrospect

How easy it was to miss
that bloom in the man's garden at Warnock's Cross,
the rare orchid *Spiranthes romanzoffiana*;

impossible to guess
the silence, among the heirlooms of the McClintocks,
of Haydn's lost Mass.

At the Smugglers' Restaurant, Carrickfergus

On three sides the windows are full of the sea.
We sit suspended in a glass of light
and wind-blown water half the afternoon,
each other's best company, though we include
the Venus on the sill, her nakedness
one veil away and she includes herself
in our least silence.
                    And everything that moves
between here and the horizon completes, upbraids
our least stillness:
speed-boats deft with purpose, unflappable freighters,
delicate yachts hovering on one wing.

The Photograph

We stop for a field of sunflowers
in the Dardanelles, an hour from Anzac Cove,
a coastal carnival in golds and greens
that bursts from the Aegean and runs waving
along the road to Troy.

And we who have travelled silent, too much subdued
by seaside graves, a field of lectern stones
in neat terraces, by place as elegy
and the nothing you could put a face to
we call death,

are glad of what turns naturally to the sun,
this crop of blank faces nature left
on floppily human heads. How can we fail
to miss their focus — a presence so much more
than past-meets-future?

As you are, love, on whom I focus now
for this group portrait. Cheek to cheek you stand
with a whole field of sunflowers. They yearn so near
you could put your arms around them, these huge, blind,
flamboyant creatures, craving your face, your smile.

The Charlotte Gibson Bed

Men have streets named after them and housing estates.
The ghost of Charlotte Gibson, whoever she was,
is nowhere around. Her plaque shines from the wall
with love too practical for other words
than name and gift: *The Charlotte Gibson Bed*.
Big-boned, austere, adjustable, it folds you in,
your mobile home for the week. Tonight a gale
howls from its prehistoric loneliness
between lough and mountain. Remember the night of storm
we sat up late and named our beloved dead?
My half-self, sleepless in our half-empty bed
invokes it now, its closeness and its fear,
between you and all harm.
Turns with you, catching echoes from the ward
that might be laughter or the worst possible news.
The grief of women, a hidden century's pain
embedded beyond earshot, the unimagined cries
that broke in silence, gather as desperate rain.
Though watching the first light's way with rain
at the bedroom window, I want you to open your eyes,
if not on raindrops, at least where light can choose
a durable reflection. Let them uncloud,
letter by letter, on a woman's name,
the brass plaque that bears whoever she was
into our story — not the first or last
to be grateful for the Charlotte Gibson Bed.

A Paris Honeymoon

1 *L'Orangerie*

We have floated to the surface of Monet's pond
this morning in the Orangerie, somewhere among
discarded buttonholes, bedraggled bouquets,
the wreaths of drowned sorrows.
Your face grows secret and lovely. It is a face
of many fathoms in this time and place.
I am the lover opening his eyes
in mid-kiss, as though he might surprise
the unique swirl of self, who catches instead,
buoyant and timeless and all unaware,
you crossing, perhaps, your exact instant of death,
too brimmed with love and living to yield it room
for this or many a year — or you submerged
in the not-yet-carnate moment of giving birth.
Primordial blossoms. Watery nebulae.
Blurred, breathless features in a spawny hush
gathering towards us, miming the kiss of light.

2 Notre-Dame

Everyone has the same secret. Now we know.
We have been ascending all our lives to
reach this place: the bell-tower of Notre-Dame.
Clearly the guide wonders what took us so long
and why we are breathless.
He bullies us gently under the iron rim,
his voice — *messieurs, mesdames* — the softest breeze
that ever touched our faces. Can we tell
how many steps? His fingers climb the air.
How wide the bell? How heavy? When he sings
a love song lightly, as into a dark well's
inverted silence, or strokes the bell's lips,
whatever is held unclenches, whatever mute
unnerves its timbre.
Spellbound, we pluck at the uncatchable,
miss as we should. Nothing is banal
between earth and heaven,
the hands summoned to reverence,
the tongue founded for love.

3 *Versailles*

It is there like a gift from the blue, the one cloud
making light of its shadow, a sun-edged
straggler from a stormy day elsewhere in Europe.
As it drifts towards Africa in the time it might take
to infect its welcome, we watch it taking its time:
the dithery ghost of a downpour, a thundery past
ruffling what had become the clear sky's
too-troubling perfection.
May it find the Atlas Mountains or a parched
trough in the dunes and rain to its heart's content.
Here, distance grows intimate, as though the day
resolved in us its long perspectives.
While we, the sum of all our weathers, stroll
in a cloud-crossed garden
or stand in freshened light beside a lake
cloud-deep in memories.

4 *Le Père Lachaise*

Ten francs will buy you a map of the underground,
your aid to orienteering among the dead.
Stopping to take your bearings — you are here,
and here, and here — on the jostling avenues,
you'd almost think death had called it a day,
its gathering of gifted lifetimes all but complete.
This morning, from the cemetery of the Jews
to the crematorium's archive of ashes,
from Héloïse and Abélard to the wall
where the last communards perished,
celebrity-spotters, pilgrims, we renew
all that the dead bequeath and we inherit,
all that is endless above and under the earth.
We might stay longer but choose our time to go,
not flirting with the darker cemetery gods
that sit at noon and feed on shadows.
The map folds easily, more than souvenir.
Angels, stone widows watch us, hand in hand,
past the last tombstone, the funeral at the gate,
not looking back and never to return.

Open House

for Karen

The house for you! Mature accommodation,
    No longer haunted, easy with the past,
Lived in before and needing renovation,
    But warm and dry, my darling, built to last.
Plumbing a little noisy, kitchen as new,
Combined reception/bedrooms, each with a view.

It's yours! You are its extra dimension,
    Light at its windows, what the future meant
From the first brick, a natural extension,
    Best, final, most desirable resident.
Your house-hunting days are over, love — so come,
Take full possession, make yourself at home.

Three Cradle Songs

1

for Matthew Rogers
b. 29 December 1989

The world is six days old.
He lies in white
in a white room
and January light
attends his cradle.
We watch his restful face
come into its own.

Will he open his eyes?
In his own sweet time he will,
on us, on the Cavehill —
old head-in-the-mist
dreaming blues and greens
a mile from his window,
his first present of spring.

2

for David Rogers
b. 5 April 1993

The spirit of Lent is broken. On holiday
for the first time in years,
he finds in us his happy hour.
The raising of his glass
is a lost art recovered.
His Easter self
sleeps in Maternity,

will wake to the name David,
treating his kin
(exhausted in all but loving,
schooled in love
by his tearaway elder)
to the best gift of this or any season:
a new place and reason for love to begin.

3

for Paul Rogers
b. 20 June 1995

Darkness is in retreat
and light is the word.
The days stay out till midnight,
their warmth preserved
at open windows.
In a family for all seasons
the summer is his.

Always the sun slants closer,
cornering the shade
where he sleeps in the back garden
to the sounds of home.
His womb-tanned head
feeds on his brothers' voices.
He yawns and stretches and our lives make room.

Lullaby

Blastocyst, little worm,
for what it's worth,
your winter womb-life
in the stormy north
basks in the prospect
of a summer birth.
Our bed is warm,
we promise you the earth.

The Heart

In your sixth week the talk is all of peace,
the killing goes on. The city you will call home
aspires to be the capital of bereavement.
Its people perfect the art of dressing up
to follow coffins and the wild grief
of women and children is a sign of the times.
We barely know the place. If you could raise
your little antennae for an early scan,
what would you find? That the sky has been lost for days
in a bad dream of rain settling for good;
Cavehill a swamped profile that has returned
to the amniotic marsh. That peace is all talk
and the killing goes on.

No face as yet, but in a Belfast street
of late-night shoppers, or the passenger seat,
or your mother's classroom, your heart begins to beat.

You: The Movie

We peer through drizzle
on a twelve-inch screen.
Your one-inch shadow
stirs behind the grain.
You are the new star
swum into our ken.
You are, you will be,
may be, might have been.

The bounds of possibility
in one
unfocussed image. The cave
of the unborn —
a silent classic,
a chiaroscuro pan
through ghostly footage
primitive as dawn.

Outside, the window
gathers Arctic showers.
Your photogenic heart
within its layers
is, meanwhile, stealing
the show. No carking cares.
It throbs and throbs
at twice the speed of ours.

The Names

The sport we had, choosing a name for you.
What long-shots and near misses and speculative lobs.
What letter-games, exuberant *A*s to *Z*s
in the big wrought-iron bed.

The sounds that will mean *you* all the days of your life.
Nothing rococo, simple harmonies
to go with affection, not out of tune with love.

Your gnomic poise so absolute you might
be playing hide-and-seek with oblivion,
we call and call again —
Helen and Paul and Peter and Louise —
into your silence. Imagine them relayed
mysteriously as greetings, promises,
how you liked the sound of one of them and stayed.

Audience Participation

We had not thought to find
you on the move
with such aplomb,
so quirkily alive.
Spotlit, at fifteen weeks,
once more you give
the performance of your life.
We script it with love.

Look at the head, we say,
as though a head
were the first mould for the planet.
Who ever played
so well
the comic lead
in such a drama?
Laughing, we applaud
ourselves in your image,
reflected, remade.

The Crossing

When there's black ice your mother takes my arm.
We make a clumsy ballet of our care.
Watching our step, we shelter you from harm.

We two, you slung between us, are a charm
proof against winter. We heat the wintriest air.
When there's black ice your mother takes my arm.

Sleep in your bones. A sleep without alarm
becomes you best, unbroken, unaware.
Watching our step, we shelter you from harm.

But should you wake, riding this little storm,
let's shape a rite of passage we can share.
When there's black ice your mother takes my arm.

We strike a three-way balance fit to disarm
whatever dangers edge the approaching shore.
Watching our step, we shelter you from harm.

The fourth month of your crossing, dark rains swarm
down from the mountain, the trees are winter-bare.
When there's black ice your mother takes my arm.
Watching our step, we shelter you from harm.

The Easter Ceasefire

The week began with blood-drops, stains more than blood,
on a bathroom tissue, a tense, suspended day
when it seemed you had stopped moving. Between pains,
less pains than twinges, your mother curled in bed,
hugging the inverted hammock of herself
where you slept or played possum. You kicked again
languidly next morning but, better safe,
we drove to the hospital and there you were,
placidly active, insouciantly unaware
on the small screen. Outside there was snow falling,
sleet more than snow, the spring so day-to-day
it had no sense of weather to call its own.
The doctor advised rest, so, better safe
from gales and rough crossings, we stayed at home,
our planned break receding like the raw
wind-note in the chimney. That was how we survived
the Easter ceasefire. Three days without blood.
A housebound, phantom holiday where spring
had failed to happen and all the ferries sailed
at odd hours, between storms; where snowflakes fell
on Windermere and Grasmere and the slopes of Skiddaw,
big, comforting dollops there was no mistaking
as the real thing. In the fraught silence between
might-be and might-have-been,
we edged towards Saturday and the hoped-for all-clear.

St Valentine's Day

No wonder you scratch
your head. Somewhere below,
that red-hot, tireless
pace-maker on the go
as though there were
no tomorrow, keeps telling you,
slow coach, you've got some
catching up to do.

Travellers

Call us your guides.
Excited and afraid,
we cross your city
seven days ahead.
We scan the unknown
as though it might be made
safe to receive you,
sufficient to your need.

The routes proliferate,
all leading west.
Your guides are suspect —
half the time they are lost.
The place belongs to no one,
in its dust
ten million prints,
the ghosts of travellers past.

It scarcely matters.
Travelling as we must
we'll guide each other,
following the rest.
This is no time
to reason with the worst.
Our best intentions
match your casual trust.

Come as You Are

You are nobody's bid for perfection.
Come as you are.
Not as a promise,
not as hope and heir
of the new century
or trammelled with any care.
No weight of expectation.
Come as you are
when your day and hour beckon.
We'll take it from there.

Helen

b. 12 August 1994

The war will soon be over, or so they say.
Five floors below the Friday rush-hour starts.
You're out and breathing. We smile to hear you cry.
Your long fingers curl around our hearts.

The place knows nothing of you and is home.
Indifferent skies look on while August warms
the middle air. We wrap you in your name.
Peace is the way you settle in our arms.

Acknowledgements

Acknowledgements are due to the editors of the following in which some of these poems were published first: *Aquarius, Belfast Newsletter, Causeway, Edinburgh Review, Foolscap, Fortnight, The Honest Ulsterman, The Independent, The Irish Times, New Statesman, Quarry, The Spark, The Sunday Times, Verse, Confounded Language: New Poems by Nine Irish Writers*, with images by Noel Connor (Bloodaxe), *The Poetry Book Society Anthology 1986-87, Living Landscape Anthology*, with drawings by Cóilín Murray (West Cork Arts Centre), *Robert Greacen: A Tribute at the Age of Seventy* (Poetry Ireland), *At Six O'Clock in the Silence of Things: A Festschrift for James Simmons* (Lapwing), *The Great Book of Ireland* and *Modern Irish Poetry: An Anthology* (Blackstaff).